THE FLYING TRUNK

and Other Stories from Hans Andersen

Retold by Naomi Lewis

Prentice-Hall Books for Young Readers

A Division of Simon & Schuster, Inc.
New York

Published by Prentice-Hall Books For Young Readers
A Division of Simon & Schuster, Inc.
Simon & Schuster Building
1230 Avenue of the Americas
New York, New York 10020

PRENTICE-HALL BOOKS FOR YOUNG READERS
is a trademark of Simon & Schuster, Inc.
Published in Great Britain by Andersen Press Ltd.

Printed by Grafiche AZ, Italy

10 9 8 7 6 5 4 3 2 1
Library of Congress Cataloging-in-Publication Data

Lewis, Naomi.
  The flying trunk and other stories from
Hans Andersen.

  Summary: Retells thirteen fairy tales by the
Danish author, including "The Tinderbox,"
"The Steadfast Tin Soldier," "The Little Match
Girl," and "The Snowman."
  1. Fairy tales—Denmark.   2. Children's stories,
Danish—Translations into English.   3. Children's
stories, English—Translations from Danish.
[1. Fairy tales.   2. Short stories]
I. Andersen, H. C. (Hans Christian), 1805–1875.
Tales.   English.   Selections.   II. Title.

PZ8.L4812fl   1987   [E]   86–25338
ISBN 0–13–322546–1

CONTENTS

Introduction

By his own reckoning Andersen left a total of 156 stories, though only a few of these—scarcely a quarter of that number—are widely known. The artists in this book, however, have chosen from the entire range, avoiding only, for practical reasons, the very long tales. As it happens, their choice has included several familiar stories, some less so, and two or three that will probably not be known. Each one, of course, is seen from an illustrator's view. But each one tells us also something about the teller himself, for he put some mark or sign of himself in almost every tale. Wait—we'll be coming to that.

It could be said that the strangest Andersen tale of all is the true one. This begins with a very poor boy, born in 1805 in a small country far to the north, a land whose language was hardly known outside its frontiers. And yet this boy, the washerwoman's crazy son as the local people called him, was to become in his lifetime the best-known and best-loved Dane in all the world. And so he still remains.

How did this come about? Through his gift for inventing stories, and for telling them in such a way that each reader seems the special and private listener. It made him an honored guest (and reader-aloud) in the royal courts of Europe, for little kingdoms abounded in that vanished yesterday. He had as a child one piece of luck. His shoemaker father, who died when his son was eleven, was not much good at the trade he had to follow, but he was a reader and thinker with quite advanced ideas. He used to take the little boy into the woods, and point out the grass blades, flowers and insects, each with a life of its own. He also made toy theaters with cut-out characters, and his son became unusually skilled, all his life, with scissors and paper—see *The Steadfast Tin Soldier* with its paper castle and fragile paper dancer. What Andersen the writer learned from this was that everything in life can be told and acted in miniature through plants and toys and pots and pans and the contents of a rubbish bin. Everything, if you have the eye to see, has its human personality. And this was a special feature of Andersen's work, as several stories here can demonstrate. Edward Lear and Lewis Carroll are among the few originals with a similar vision. But the followers of Andersen, some at the highest level of writing, have been legion.

The road to success was a hard one. Go back for a moment to Andersen at fourteen, a yellow-haired scarecrow, newly arrived in Copenhagen, dancing, singing, a starving hopeful, persistently knocking at influential doors, until a group of responsible people collected a fund and sent him off to be educated.

There, a great tall misfit between cruel small boys and a cruel headmaster with whom he had to lodge, he suffered much. But he obtained his degree at last and chose to become a writer. He thought of himself as the author of plays and novels for adults, but the real response came from a small group of fairy tales published in 1835. The first two of these are in this book. He wrote a few more the next year, and the next, and realized that everything he might wish to say could be said through this new medium. By the end of his life (in 1875) he was known in translation all through the reading world.

What do we find of all this in the tales of the artists' choice? *The Tinderbox* and *The Princess and the Pea* were the opening two in the first small volume of 1835. Both were based, he tells us, on stories that he had heard as a child from women working in the spinning room or at hop-gathering. But (he added) he told them in his own way, and sure enough, they are in the unmistakable Andersen manner that holds us from the start. We are *there* with that soldier on the road; we are *down* that hollow tree. After that start he felt no more need to draw on older fairy tales; his inventions are his own.

The Emperor's New Clothes (1836) belongs to his second little collection. It is, of course, about people's readiness to believe what they are told, to follow what other people are doing and saying instead of looking honestly at the facts. That's happening still, and a very bad thing it is! Many artists have tried their hand at illustrating this story and dealing with its saucy problem in any number of ways. Here is another!

The Steadfast Tin Soldier (1838), a top favorite with everyone and rightly so, is a real original invention, a good example too of a dramatic and moving story told through *things*. Many people wrote that they had been helped in trouble by reading of the soldier's endurance and courage. The passport episode echoes a familiar worry of Andersen's. He loved traveling, but found passports and such a continual anxiety. As for the paper castle and little dancer, he would create for you these and other fancies if ever you chanced to meet him.

The Flying Trunk (1839) is a particularly interesting story. The magical notion of flying through the air, and thereby discovering a princess, had long been around in fairy tale: but where the Arabian Nights provided a magic carpet or flying horse, Andersen typically substitutes an old trunk, very much, I imagine, like the one he used himself. Perhaps he was looking at it as he wrote. As for the storyteller, so warmly welcomed by royalty, that, as we know, was no make-believe. And the tale itself, that so greatly pleased the young man's kind royal hosts, of kitchen things arguing, boasting, gossiping, you can read there Andersen's own real views on the pompous and disapproving people who never looked beyond their own small scene.

The Swineherd (1842) is a play on the theme of not recognizing quality; the naturally gifted nightingale is despised when set against the expensive mechanical model. But there are other things in that story too. *The Top and the Ball* (1845)—another excellent human story told through things—is, as likely as not, based on a personal experience. But the fiction writer can turn life to his will! *The Jumping Competition* (1847), "told on the spur of the moment to some children who asked for a story" is, if you like, about the wrong people winning the prizes, for the wrong reasons too. And that has a truth for everybody even perhaps the winners. *The Little Match Girl* (1848), a real Christmas heartbreaker, needs no commentary. We are told, though, that it was based on a picture.

Three of the remaining four—two light invented fables with a distinct message in each, and a mysterious piece that holds its own secrets, *From the Ramparts of the Citadel* (1857)—are the least known of all in the book. The fourth, *The Snowman* (1861), a not very well-known tale with a curious twist at the end, is one that tells you more each time you read it. It also happens to be the only one in this book which brings out Andersen's marvelous power of suggesting weather and seasons in words alone. Impossible to forget are the brilliant, freezing snow and ice, so welcome to the snowman, so enchanting to the lovers in their brief walk through the white and sparkling trees, so hard on the ill-used dog, with its hoarse and cynical wisdom—followed at last by the sudden lovely sense of spring, that melts the pang of the snowman's vanishing.

Every Andersen story is a living picture, a series of pictures that live, through words, in the mind. For over a century and a half, artists have made illustrations for these tales, and every vision is different. Yet, apart from the black and white drawings made by Pedersen and Frølich in Andersen's lifetime, there are no illustrations, certainly none in color, that are lastingly linked with Andersen's text.

Thirteen leading artists have set out to match their skill and imagination to the work of the Danish master, in the fairy tale of their choice. They come from many countries. Their very diverse visions add to the book's excitement.

Naomi Lewis
London, September 1986

The Tinderbox

—— Illustrated by ——

Tomie dePaola

Asoldier came marching down the road—Left, right! Left, right! He had a pack on his back and a sword at his side; he had been in the wars, and was now on his way home. Along the road he met a witch. She was a frightful sight! Her lower lip hung down almost to her waist.

"Hallo, young soldier," said the witch. "That's a handsome sword you have, and a fine knapsack too. You're a proper soldier, no mistake! Do you want money? I'll show you how to get as much money as you want."

"Thanks very much, old witch," said the soldier.

"Do you see that big tree?" said the witch. She was pointing to a tree just beside them. "It's quite hollow inside. If you climb up to the top of the trunk you'll see a hole, and you can slide down that to the bottom. I'll tie a rope around your waist so that I can pull you up when you call."

"What am I supposed to do down there?" said the soldier.

"Fetch the money, that's what," said the witch. "Now listen to me. When you get to the bottom you'll find yourself in a long passage. It's perfectly light, because over a hundred lamps are kept burning there. You'll see three doors; they'll be easy to open because the keys are in the locks. Start in the first room. You'll find a great wooden chest in the middle of the floor with a dog sitting on it. The dog has eyes as big as teacups—but don't let that bother you. Here, I'm giving you my blue-checked apron. Spread it out on the floor, lift the dog on to it—no, don't be afraid—then you can open the chest and take as much money as you like out of it. It is all coppers, I must tell you. If you'd rather have silver you must go into the next room. You'll find a dog there with eyes as big as millstones, but don't let that worry you. Just lift the box, put it on the apron and help yourself. If it's gold you are after, though, you can get that in the third room, as much as you can carry. But the dog there has eyes as big as the Round Tower. That's a dog of dogs, you won't see his like anywhere else in this world, I can tell you. But never you mind about that. Just put him on to my apron and he won't do you any harm. Then take as much gold as you like."

"That doesn't sound so bad!" said the soldier. "But tell me, old witch, what's in all this for yourself? You can't be doing it for nothing."

"I don't want a single penny," said the witch. "All you need do for me is collect a dusty old tinderbox that my grandmother forgot when she was last down there."

"Don't let's waste any more time," said the soldier. "Give me the rope; I'll tie it around my middle."

"Here it is," said the witch. "And here's my blue-checked apron."

The soldier climbed up the tree and slid down the hole. Thump! He found himself in a great passage, just as the witch had said.

He unlocked the first door. My, my, my! There sat the dog with eyes as big as teacups; it stared and glared at him.

"You're a nice little fellow," said the soldier. He lifted the dog on to the witch's apron and crammed his pockets with coppers. Then he shut the lid, put the dog back on top and marched into the second room. There sat the dog with eyes as big as millstones.

"You shouldn't stare so hard," said the soldier. "You'll strain your eyes." And he lifted the dog on to the apron. But when he saw the masses of silver coins, he threw away all the coppers and filled his pockets and knapsack too with silver.

Then he went into the third room. This was really frightful! The dog there had eyes as large as the great Round Tower, and they went around and around in its head like wheels.

"Good evening," said the soldier, and he touched his cap politely, for he had never seen a dog like that before. But after he had stared at the creature for a while, he said to himself, "Enough of that!" Then he heaved the dog on to the apron, and lifted the lid of the chest. Heavens! What heaps of gold! It was enough to buy the whole of Copenhagen, as well as all the sugar pigs, tin soldiers, spinning tops and rocking horses in the world. Yes, that was money all right. Quickly he threw away all the silver coins in his pockets and knapsack and stuffed them with gold instead; then he filled his cap, and after that his boots. Indeed, he could hardly walk! Now for once he really had money. He lifted the dog back on its box, slammed the door behind him and shouted up the tree,

"Hi, old witch! Pull me up again!"

"Have you got the tinderbox?" asked the witch.

"Bless me, old dame, you're right," said the soldier. "It had slipped my mind."

And he went back and collected it. The witch hauled him up, and there he stood in the road once more, but now with pockets, cap, knapsack and boots all bulging out with gold.

"Why do you want the tinderbox?" asked the soldier.

"That's no business of yours," said the witch. "You've got your money; just give me the tinderbox. That was the arrangement."

"Oh, rubbish," said the soldier. "Tell me what you are going to do with it, or I'll cut off your head with my sword."

"No," said the witch. "You're wasting your time."

But she was wrong. The soldier cut off her head and there she lay. The soldier put all his gold in her apron, tied it into a bundle and threw it over his shoulder. Then he slipped the tinderbox into his pocket and strode off into the town.

It was a fine town, and the soldier made for the finest inn where he booked the very best rooms and ordered all his favorite things to eat. He was a rich man now! The servant whose job it was to clean his boots thought, "Funny old boots for such a grand customer"—but the soldier soon put that right. Next day he went out and bought expensive boots and plenty of fine new clothes. He was a proper gentleman now, and people were glad to tell him all about the town, its sights and pleasures, and about the king and the lovely princess his daughter.

"I wouldn't mind seeing her," said the soldier.

"Not a hope," he was told. "She lives in a big copper castle, with walls and towers all around. No one is allowed to visit except her parents. You see, it has been prophesied that she will marry a common soldier and the king won't put up with that."

The soldier was now living a merry sort of life. He went to the theater; he drove in his own carriage through the park, and he gave away handfuls of money to the poor. He hadn't forgotten what it was like to be poor himself. How pleasant it was to be rich and well-dressed! Friends flocked around, all telling him what a splendid fellow he was, a real gentleman. He liked that, you may be sure. But as he was spending money all the time and never earning anything, a day came when he found that he had only two pennies left. He was obliged to leave his grand apartment and move into a cramped little attic under the roof. He had not only to clean his own boots, but to mend them too; he did this with a darning needle. None of his former friends ever called; they didn't want to climb all those stairs.

One evening, when he was sitting in the dark since he couldn't afford a candle, he suddenly remembered that there was a candle-end in the tinder box, the one he had brought from the hollow tree. But the moment he struck the flint to make a light, the door flew open and there, before him, was the dog with eyes as big as teacups. "What are my lord's commands?" said the dog.

"I say, that's an odd sort of tinderbox," thought the soldier. "Can I have whatever I want?" Aloud, he said to the dog, "Bring me some money." Flick! It was gone. Flack! It was back—with a bag of coppers in its mouth—all in less than a second.

And now the soldier realized what a treasure he possessed. You struck the flint once, he found, for the dog with the copper coins, twice for the dog with silver, three times for the dog in charge of the gold. So, without much delay, he was back in the grand set of rooms, wearing elegant clothes. And now, of course, all his friends flocked back; they couldn't get enough of his company.

One day he thought to himself, "It's very odd that no one

can see the princess. She's supposed to be such a beauty— but what's the good of that if she has to stay in that copper castle with all those walls and towers? There must be a way of getting through. Where's my tinderbox?" He struck the flint, and—whoosh!—there was the dog with eyes as big as teacups.

"I know it's pretty late at night," he said, "but I would like to see that princess, if only for half a minute."

The dog was gone in a flash, and just as quickly returned with the princess fast asleep on his back. Oh, she was lovely, a real princess, no doubt about that. The soldier couldn't resist the chance of giving her a kiss; after all, he was a real soldier. But the half minute was soon gone, and the dog sped back to the castle with the sleeping girl. In the morning though, at breakfast with her father and mother, she told them that she had had a very strange dream. A great dog had taken her on a lightning ride, and a soldier had kissed her.

"That's a peculiar story, I must say," said the king.

Now one of the older ladies-in-waiting was told to sit by the princess's bed next night to see if she had another dream of the same sort—and to see if it *was* a dream. And as it happened, the soldier longed so much for another sight of the princess that on that night he again sent the dog to collect her, and the dog did what he was asked. But the lady-in-waiting was on the alert; she put on her galoshes, followed the dog at a racing speed, and when she saw it vanish with her charge in a big house she said to herself, "Now we'll know the truth of the matter!" And she chalked a cross on the door. Then she went back to get some sleep.

But the dog was no fool. When it saw a chalked cross on the soldier's door it took a bit of chalk and put crosses on all the doors in the town. That was clever of him, because now she hadn't a chance of finding the place.

Next morning, the king and queen and a host of court

officials were taken by the lady-in-waiting to see the house with the mark.

"Here it is!" said the king, catching sight of a door with a cross.

"No, husband, it's here," said the queen as she looked at another door.

"There's another!" "There's another!" they were all now saying. And soon they realized that it was no use trying to find the right house; they might just as well go home.

But the queen—ah, she was a clever one. She could do more than just ride about in a glittering carriage. She took up her big golden scissors, cut up a piece of silk and sewed it into a pretty little bag. This she filled with very fine grains of buckwheat. Then she fastened the bag to her daughter's back, and snipped a little hole in the silk so that grains would trickle out and mark the path. That night the dog came again, took the princess and sped with her to the soldier; he was now so much in love that he longed to be a prince and so be able to marry her. But the dog never noticed the trail of grain all the way from the castle to the soldier's window. When morning came it was plain enough to the king and queen where their daughter had been. They had the soldier seized and put in prison.

There he sat in a dark and wretched cell. And the jailors kept saying to him, "Tomorrow you're to be hanged." He didn't enjoy that at all. The worst of it was, he had left his tinderbox in his room. In the first light of morning he looked through the iron bars of the little window; there were crowds, all hurrying past to see him hanged. Drums were sounding for the event; soldiers were marching briskly. Everyone was rushing to get a good view. Quite near, he saw a cobbler's boy in leather apron and slippers; he was scurrying along so fast that one of his slippers flew off and struck the wall where the soldier was peering out behind the bars.

"I say, you cobbler's boy," said the soldier. "You don't have to hurry; they can't begin without me. Wait though—if you'll run along to my place and fetch my tinderbox, you'll have something for yourself. But you'll have to be quick!" The boy was only too glad to earn a coin or two, and raced off. He was soon back with the tinderbox, gave it to the soldier and—well, listen carefully, and you'll know what happened.

Outside the town a gallows had been built. Around it stood the soldiers, crowded behind were thousands and thousands of people. The king and queen sat on a splendid throne; the judges and councilors sat directly opposite. As for the soldier, he had already climbed the ladder to the platform; but just as they were going to put the rope around his neck, and there was a moment's silence, he called out,

"Don't forget the custom: anyone about to be hanged is allowed a last small request, and mine's a little one. I just want to smoke a pipe of tobacco, my last in this world."

The king couldn't very well say no to that, so the soldier took out the tinderbox to strike a light. One! Two! Three! he struck. And there stood all three dogs, the one with eyes as big as teacups, the one with eyes like millstones, and the third with eyes as huge as the Round Tower.

"Now you three, save me from being hanged!" said the soldier. At once the dogs leapt upon the judges and councilors, seizing some by the legs and some by the nose, and tossed them into the air. When they came down they were dashed to pieces.

"Not me—I won't be tossed!" cried the king. But the biggest dog picked up both king and queen and sent them hurtling into the air like the others. The guards and soldiers were terrified, but the people were delighted with the fun. They called out, "Little soldier, you be our king and marry the princess!" They lifted the soldier into the royal carriage and the three dogs frisked about in front, barking in their

17

own way, "Hurrah! Hurrah!" The urchins and young apprentices whistled through their fingers; the guards presented arms. The princess stepped down from her copper castle and became the queen. She liked that, I can tell you. The wedding feast lasted a whole week, while the three dogs sat at the table and rolled their eyes at all the other guests.

It's Absolutely True!

Illustrated by

Ruth Brown

"What a shocking business!" said a hen who lived in a part of the town quite a distance away from where the shocking thing was supposed to have taken place. "And in a henhouse too! I'm thankful there are so many of us on the perch. I wouldn't dare to sleep alone tonight."

And she told her tale. It made all the other hens' feathers stand on end, and the cock's comb fall down flat. I tell you, it's perfectly true!

But we'll begin at the beginning, and that takes us into a henhouse nowhere near the other. Here, as the sun went down, the birds flew up to roost for the night. One of them was a hen with white feathers and short legs, laying her regulation egg each day—a thoroughly respectable creature. As she settled on the perch she tidied herself with her beak, and one little feather fell out.

"Well, well," she said. "There it goes. The neater I am, the more handsome I shall be.'' She said this in fun, for she was a lively bird, fond of a joke, though in all ways, as I have said, most respectable. And then she settled herself to sleep.

Darkness fell. Along the perch in the henhouse all the birds slept but one—that was the next door neighbor of the one who had lost her feather. She heard, and she did not hear—always the best thing to do if you want to live peacefully. And yet, she could not resist nudging her other neighbor. "Did you hear that?" she whispered. "I name no names, but there's a hen in this very place who wants to pluck out her feathers to look attractive. If I were the cock, I'd despise that creature!"

Just above the henhouse lived an owl family, two parent owls and their children. Like all owls they had sharp ears, and heard every word that was being said below. They rolled their eyes and the mother owl shook her wings. "Don't listen!" she said. "Still, I expect you heard all the same. I heard it with my own ears, and they are not likely to fall off. Fancy! One of the hens has so far forgotten how to behave that she's plucking out all her feathers, in full view of the cock!"

"*Prenez garde aux enfants!*" said the father owl. "That's no talk for children to hear."

"Well, I'll just tell the owl over the way. She's such a respectable bird, she'll want to hear," said the mother owl. And off she flew.

"Tu whoo! Tu whoo!" she called to the pigeons in the nearby roost. "Have you heard? Have you heard? Tu whoo!—There's a hen who has plucked out all her feathers for love of the cock. She must be freezing to death, if she isn't dead already. Tu whoo!"

"Where? Where?" cooed the pigeons.

"In the yard over there. I almost saw it myself. It's hardly a fit story to tell, but it's absolutely true!"

"Coo, coo, it's really true," said the pigeons, and they passed on the tale to their own henhouse. "There's a hen—some say two—who plucked out all her feathers to catch the eye of the cock. It was a dangerous thing to do. To dooo. You could catch cold and die, and that's what happened to the two! Coo!"

"Wake up, wake up," crowed the cock, flying on to the fence. His eyes were blurred with sleep, but he still could crow. "Three hens have died for the love of a cock! They plucked out all their feathers—a terrible story! I won't keep it to myself. You can pass it on!"

"Pass it on, pass it on," echoed the bats. The hens clucked, and the cocks crew: "Pass it on!" In this way the gossip sped from henhouse to henhouse, until it arrived back at the very place where it had started. But how it had grown! "Five hens," now ran the story, "plucked out all their feathers to see which had grown the thinnest for love of the cock. Then they pecked one another until they fell down dead—a scandal to their families and a proper loss to their owner."

The hen who had shed the loose feather certainly did not recognize herself in the monstrous story and, being a respectable bird, she said, "I do despise those creatures. But there are too many like that still around. Such doings shouldn't be hushed up. I'm going to do my best to see that it gets into the newspapers, then the whole country will know about it. Those hussies have deserved it—and their families too!"

The story did get into the papers. One thing at least is absolutely true, that a single little feather can grow overnight into five hens.

The Snowman

—————— Illustrated by ——————

Michael Foreman

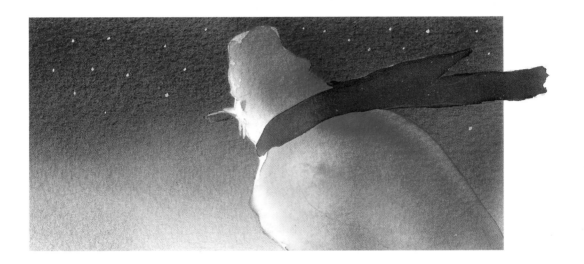

"Oh, how I crackle and crunch!" said the snow-man. "How I love the freezing cold! This icy wind stings life into a fellow, I can tell you. Ugh! Look at that hot red thing above, always glaring and staring!" (He meant the sun, which was just about to set.) "But she won't make me blink. Oh no. I can stare back."

The snowman had three-cornered pieces of tile for his two eyes, and an old rake for his mouth, so he had teeth as well. His birth had been greeted by cheers and shouts from the boys and by tinkling bells and cracking whips from the sleighs.

The sun went down and the moon rose up, a full moon, round and clear, lovely in the violet evening sky.

"There she is again, on the other side," said the snowman. He thought that the moon was the sun. "Still, at least I've stopped her glaring. All right, she's welcome to stay up there if she gives me a bit of light to see what's going on. If only I knew how to move! I do wish I could get about. If I could, I'd go down to the lake and slide on the ice, like the boys. But I don't know how to move, let alone run."

"Off! Off!" barked an old watchdog, who was chained to his kennel. His voice was hoarse now that he had to live outside. Once his home was inside the house, and he had a place near the stove.

"The sun will teach you to run," said the watchdog. "That's what happened to last year's snowman, and the one before that; I saw it, I can tell you. Off! Off! Off they've all gone."

"Sorry, friend, I don't understand you," said the snowman. "How can that thing up there teach me to run? She's the one who ran when I stared back at her. Now she's sneaking in from the other side!"

"You don't know anything," said the watchdog. "But of course you have only just been put together. The one you see up there is called the moon. The other round one is the sun, and she'll be back tomorrow. She will make you run—right down into the lake. The weather's going to change quite soon—I know from the twinge in my left hindleg."

"I don't understand him," thought the snowman. "But I have a feeling that he's telling me something unpleasant. The hot one—the sun he called her, the one that was here just now then went away—she's no friend of mine, I can feel that."

The weather did change soon. Early next morning a heavy mist filled the air. When it lifted a sharp wind rose, and everything was covered in frost. But out came the sun, and the result was magical! The hoarfrost made the forest seem like a reef of whitest coral; look again, and every tree and bush seemed thick with white and silver flowers. The delicate twigs and branches, hidden by leaves in the summer, now showed their real design. It was quite marvelous, as intricate as lace, and so brilliantly white that it seemed to send out rays of light itself. The silver birch swayed in the wind, just as it did in summer. How incredibly beautiful it was! And when the sun rose high, everything seemed to be covered with glittering diamond dust. Or, you could think that a thousand thousand tiny candles were alight, whiter than snow itself.

"How enchanting it is!" said a girl, a young lady, who had come into the garden with a young man. "Why, it is even more beautiful now than it is in summer." And her eyes sparkled like the sparkling scene.

"And you won't find a handsome fellow like that in the summer," said the young man, pointing to the snowman.

The girl laughed, and gave the snowman a friendly nod; then she and her companion went tripping across the snow, which crunched under their feet as if they were walking on starch.

"Who were those two?" the snowman asked the watchdog. "You've been here longer than I have, so I suppose you know them."

"Yes, I do," said the watchdog. "She has patted my back, and he has given me a bone. I would never bite either of them."

"Why do they walk hand-in-hand?"

"They are sweethear-r-r-rts," growled the watchdog. "They are going to share a kennel and gnaw bones together. Off! Off!"

"Are they as important as us, you and I?" asked the snowman.

"Oh yes. They belong to the family," said the watchdog. "What ignorance! You don't know much! I have to remember that you weren't born until yesterday. But age brings knowledge, and I've got both. I know everyone in the house. I've known better times, too, when I didn't have to stand here chained up and frozen through. Off! Off!"

"But the cold is delightful," said the snowman. "Do go on with your story. Only please stop rattling that chain; it disturbs me right to the core."

"Off! Off!" barked the dog. "I was a puppy once. 'What a pretty little love!' they used to say. I slept on a velvet cushion; the master himself took me on his lap, so did the mistress. My paws were wiped with embroidered handkerchiefs. They kissed me; they called me 'sweet little doggy.' But when I grew too big for all that, they passed me on to the housekeeper. She lived in the basement; you can see right into her room from where you are standing. It wasn't as elegant as the one above, but it was much more comfortable. I had my own cushion to lie on and plenty of good food; what's more I wasn't teased and dragged about by the children as I had been upstairs. And then, there was the stove in winter—the loveliest thing in the world. When it was really cold I would get right under it. I still dream of being there. Off. Off!"

"What is it like, that stove? Is it handsome? Is it anything like me?"

"You couldn't be more different," said the dog. "The stove is black as night; it has a long black neck with a brass ring around it. Underneath is the fire. It eats up wood, more and more, until flames come out of its mouth. Ah, to lie near that warmth! Until you have done that you cannot know what pleasure really is. Look through that window; you can see inside from where you are standing."

The snowman did as the dog had told him, and—yes!—he saw the stove, a black polished metal shape, with brass decorations. Through a little window at the bottom shone a glowing light; of course, this came from the fire. The strangest feeling stirred in him, something he could not understand. It was a feeling known to humans, but not to a snowman.

"Why did you leave her?" he asked the watchdog. The stove, to him, seemed a she. "How could you bear to go from such a wonderful place?"

"I had no choice in the matter," said the dog. "They threw me out, chained me up, and here I am, as you see. All I ever did was to bite one of the upstairs boys in the leg—the youngest one it was. He had kicked away the bone I was gnawing. A bone is worth a bone, I thought, and I gave him a bite in the leg. But the master and mistress put all the blame on me, and ever since then I've been chained out here in the cold. It has ruined my voice; can't you hear how hoarse I am? Off! Off! You clear off! Well, that's my story."

But the snowman had stopped listening. He was staring into the basement room where the stove stood on its four iron legs. Why, she was about the same size as himself!

"I have such a strange creaking feeling inside me," he said. "Am I never to get into that room where she lives? It isn't much to ask, but if only my wish could be granted! It's the one thing in the world that I long for, and it isn't fair that I can't seem to manage it. But I must and I will get in. I must get near to that lovely creature, even if I have to break the window."

"You'll never get in there," said the watchdog. "And if you did reach the stove, you'd be off, off, off. And gone."

"I'm as good as off already," said the snowman. "I feel as if I were breaking up, somehow."

All day long the snowman stood looking in at the window. At dusk, the room seemed even more inviting. The stove gave out a gentle glow, very different from the unkind light of the sun and moon. It was the kind of glow that only a stove full of wood can give. Whenever the little door was opened, flames came dancing out, and the snowman's face shone rose colored in their light.

"It's more than I can bear," he said. "How pretty she looks when she puts out her tongue."

The night was very long, but not for the snowman. He stood there with his own beautiful thoughts, and they froze inside his head until you could hear them crackling. In the early morning the basement windows were frozen over; they were covered with the loveliest ice flowers that any snowman could wish for—but they hid the view of the stove. The panes refused to thaw, so how could he see her? The ice crackled and crunched; it was just the kind of weather to delight a snowman, but he was not delighted. He really ought to have felt at his best, but he didn't. He was unhappy; he had lost his heart to the stove.

"That's a serious complaint for a snowman!" said the watchdog. "I had it myself, but I got over it. Off! Off! There's a change in the weather coming."

He was right. A thaw was on the way. The warmer it grew, the more the snowman dwindled. He didn't say anything; he didn't even complain, and that's a bad sign.

One morning he collapsed. Where he had been standing there was a metal rod sticking up; it was around this that the boys had built him up.

"Now I understand why he longed for the stove," said the watchdog. "The snowman had a stove-rake in his body. That's the cause of the trouble. But it's all over now. He's done with all that. Off! Off!"

And soon enough winter was over too. "Off! Off!" barked the watchdog. But the girls from the house came out and sang:

> *Sweet woodruff, flower for us now.*
> *Willow, wave your tasseled bough.*
> *Lark and cuckoo, when you sing*
> *It's goodbye winter, welcome spring.*
> *Tweet, tweet! Cuckoo! We'll sing it too!*
> *Bright sun, keep shining all day through.*

And when spring comes, who gives a thought to the snowman?

The Jumping Competition

— Illustrated by —

Susan Varley

The flea, the grasshopper and the jumping jack decided to hold a competition to see who could jump the highest. They invited all the world, and anyone else who wanted, to come and see the match. Three champion jumpers they looked when they met at the appointed place.

"Well, I will give my daughter to the one who jumps the highest," said the King. "It would be a poor affair if these people had to jump for nothing but honor."

The flea was the first to step forward. He had elegant manners and bowed to the right and left—but then he had the blood of fine young maidens in him, and was used to human society. All this made a difference.

Next came the grasshopper. He was larger in size, but he had grace and style, and wore a fine green uniform. In fact, he had worn it since his birth. He claimed, moreover, that he had connections with the land of Egypt, but was also highly esteemed in modern Denmark. Indeed (he said) he had been brought from the fields and put into a house made of playing cards—court cards, all of them—with the colored sides facing inwards. The house had doors and windows too, cut from the Queen of Hearts.

"I sing so well," he boasted, "that sixteen crickets, who have chirped away all their lives without being given a house of cards, have fretted themselves into shadows just through hearing my voice."

Both the flea and the grasshopper gave glowing accounts of themselves. Each felt very well qualified to marry a princess.

Now came the jumping jack. He was made from a goose's wishbone, two rubber bands, a little stick and a blob of sealing wax. He said nothing at all, but that showed that he was a deep thinker, or so they said. The court dog sniffed at him, which proved that he came of good family. The old councilor who had been given three decorations for keeping his mouth shut, declared that the jumping jack had the gift of prophecy; you could tell from his back whether the winter would be mild or hard, and you couldn't tell that from the back of the man who writes the weather forecasts.

"I'm not saying anything," said the old King. "But that's because I prefer to keep my thoughts to myself."

And now the match began. The flea jumped so high that nobody could see him. Then everyone said that he hadn't jumped at all, and that was most unfair. The grasshopper jumped only half as high, but he jumped right into the old King's face. "That's disgusting!" said the King.

The jumping jack sat so long without moving that people began to worry. Was he thinking? Or couldn't he jump? "I hope he's not feeling out of sorts," said the court dog, and he sniffed him once again, pushing him with his nose. "Rutsch!" The jumping jack gave a little sideways leap, and landed in the lap of the princess, who was sitting quite low down on a little golden stool.

"The highest jump is the jump up to my daughter," said

the King. "That's the whole point, after all. Besides, even to think of it needs a good head, as well as good legs. The jumping jack has both."

And so he won the princess.

"My jump was the highest," said the flea. "But what do I care! She can have the old wishbone, stick and wax and all. I know I'm the winner, but in this world you need more than skill and quality to get your rights."

He joined the army, went abroad, and they say he died in battle.

The grasshopper sat down in a ditch to reflect on the ways of the world. "You need influence," he thought, "to get anywhere. You need publicity." And he sang his own sad song, and that's where we learned this story. But just because it is in print, it doesn't have to be true.

The Emperor's New Clothes

———— Illustrated by ————

Janosch

Many years ago there lived an Emperor. He was so passionately fond of fine new clothes that he spent all his money and time on dressing up. He cared nothing for his army, nor for going to the theater, nor for driving out in his carriage among the people—except as a chance for showing off his latest outfit. He had a different coat for every hour of the day; and at times when you'd be told of other monarchs, "He's holding council," in *his* case the answer would be, "The Emperor is in his dressing room."

Life was cheerful enough in the city where he lived. Strangers were always arriving, and one day a pair of shady characters turned up; they claimed to be weavers. But the cloth they wove (so they said) wasn't only exceptionally beautiful but had magical properties; even when made into clothes it was invisible to anyone who was either unfit for his job or particularly stupid. "Excellent!" thought the Emperor. "What a chance to discover which men in my kingdom aren't fit for the posts they hold—and which are the wise ones and the fools. Yes, that stuff must be woven and made into clothes at once!" And he gave the two rogues a large sum of money so that they could start.

So the rascally pair set up two looms and behaved as if they were working hard; but actually there was nothing on the machines at all. Before long they were demanding the finest silk and golden thread; these they crammed into their own pockets, and went on moving their arms at the empty looms until far into the night.

After a time, the Emperor thought, "I really *would* like to know how they are getting on." But when he recalled that no one who was stupid, or unfit for his work, could see the cloth, he felt rather awkward about going himself. It was not that he had any doubts about his own abilities, of course—yet he felt that it might be best to send someone else for a start. After all, everyone in the city knew the special powers of the cloth; everyone was longing to find out how foolish or incompetent his neighbors were.

"I know, I'll send my honest old minister to the weavers," he decided. "He's the right man, as sensible as can be; and no one can complain about the way he does his job."

So the good old minister went into the room where the two rogues were pretending to work at the looms. "Heaven help us!" he thought, and his eyes opened wider and wider. "I can't see anything." But he kept his thoughts to himself.

The two swindlers begged him to step closer; did he not agree that the patterns were beautiful, the colors delightful? And they waved their hands at the empty looms. But though the poor old minister peered and stared, he still could see nothing, for the simple reason that nothing was there to see.

"Heavens!" he thought. "Am I really stupid after all? That has never occurred to me—and it had better not occur to anyone else! Am I really unfit for my office? No—it will never do to say that I can't see any cloth."

"Well, don't you admire it?" said one of the false weavers, still moving his hands. "You haven't said a word!"

"Oh—it's charming, quite delightful," said the poor old minister, peering through his spectacles. "The pattern—the colors—yes, I must tell the Emperor that I find them truly remarkable."

"Well that's very encouraging," said the two weavers, and they pointed out the details of the pattern and the different colors worked into it. The old minister listened carefully so that he could repeat it all to the Emperor. And this he did.

The two imposters now asked for a further supply of money, silk and golden thread; they had to have it, they said, to finish the cloth. But everything that they were given went straight into their own pockets; not a stitch appeared on the looms. Yet they went on busily moving their hands at the empty machines.

Presently the Emperor sent another honest official to see how the weaving was going on, and if the stuff would soon be ready. The same thing happened to him as to the minister; he looked and looked, but as there was nothing there but the empty looms, nothing was all he saw.

"Isn't it lovely material?" said the cheats. And they held out the imaginary stuff before him, pointing out the pattern which didn't exist.

"I don't believe that I'm stupid," thought the official. "I suppose I'm really not the right man for my job. Well, I should never have thought it! And nobody else had better think it, either." So he made admiring noises about the cloth he could not see, and told the men that he was particularly pleased with the colors and design. "Yes," he reported to the Emperor, "it's magnificent."

The news of the remarkable stuff was soon all around the town. And now the Emperor made up his mind to see it while it was still on the looms. So, with a number of carefully chosen attendants—among them the two honest officials who had already been there—he went to the weaving room, where the rogues were performing their antics as busily as ever.

"What splendid cloth!" said the old minister. "Observe the design, Your Majesty! Observe the colors!" said the worthy official. And they pointed to the empty looms, for they were sure that everyone else could see the material.

"This is terrible!" thought the Emperor. "I can't see a thing! Am I stupid? Am I unfit to be Emperor? That is too frightful to think of." "Oh, it is charming, charming," he said aloud. "It has our highest approval." He nodded in a satisfied way towards the empty looms; on no account must he admit that he saw nothing there at all.

And the courtiers with him stared there too, each one with secret alarm at seeing not a single thread. But aloud they echoed the Emperor's words: "Charming, charming!" And they advised him to use the splendid cloth for a new set of royal robes he would wear for a great procession taking place in the near future. "It is magnificent, so unusual . . . ." Yes, you could hear such words all around. And the Emperor gave each of the imposters a knightly decoration to hang in his buttonhole, and the title of Imperial Court Official of the Loom.

All through the night before the procession day, the rogues pretended to work, with sixteen candles around them. Everyone could see how busy they were, trying to get the Emperor's outfit finished in time. They pretended to take the stuff from the looms; they cut away in the air with big tailor's scissors; they stitched and stitched with needles that had no thread; and at last they announced: "The clothes are ready!"

The Emperor came with his noblest courtiers to look, and the two imposters held up their arms as if lifting something. "Here are the trousers," they said. "Here is the jacket, here is the cloak"—and so on. "They are as light as gossamer; you

would think, from the feel, that you had nothing on at all—
but that, of course, is the beauty of it."

"Yes, indeed," said all the attendants; but they could not
see anything, for there was nothing there to see.

"If Your Imperial Majesty will graciously take off the
clothes you are wearing, we shall have the honor of putting on
the new ones here in front of the great mirror."

The Emperor took off his clothes, and the rogues pretended
to hand him the new set, one item at a time. They then put
their arms about his waist, and appeared to be fastening his
train, the final touch.

The Emperor turned about and twisted before the glass.
"How elegant it looks! What a perfect fit!" the courtiers
murmured. "What rich material! What splendid colors!
Have you ever seen such magnificence?"

"Your Majesty," said the Chief Master of Ceremonies, "the
canopy waits outside." The canopy was to be borne over his
head in the procession.

"Well," said the Emperor. "I am ready. It really is an
excellent fit, don't you think?" And he turned himself around
again once more in front of the mirror, as if taking a final
look. The courtiers who were to carry the train stooped, as if
to lift something from the floor, then raised their hands
before them. They were not going to let people think that
they saw nothing there.

So the Emperor walked in stately procession under the
splendid canopy; and everyone in the streets or at the
windows exclaimed, "Doesn't the Emperor look magnificent!
Those new clothes—aren't they marvelous! Just look at the
train! The elegance of it!"

For nobody dared to admit that he couldn't see any clothes;
this would have meant that he was a fool or no good at his job.
None of the Emperor's gorgeous outfits had ever been so
much admired.

Then a child's puzzled voice was clearly heard. "He's got nothing on!" "These innocents! What ridiculous things they say!" said the child's father. But the whisper passed through the crowd: "That child there says that the Emperor has nothing on; the Emperor has nothing on!"

And presently, everyone there was repeating, "He's got nothing on!" At last, it seemed to the Emperor too that they must be right. But he thought to himself, "I must not stop or it will spoil the procession." So he marched on even more proudly than before, and the courtiers continued to carry a train that was not there at all.

It is You the Fable is About

——————— Illustrated by ———————

David McKee

The wise men of ancient times had a cunning way of telling people the truth about themselves without seeming rude. They set before them a kind of mirror in which animals and other wonderful creatures appeared as in a play—and very entertaining it was to watch. Yet very few watchers or listeners knew that they were being taught a lesson. These little tales or plays were known as fables; whatever wise or foolish things the animals were made to do were really an acting out of human ways of behavior. So,

when people met one of these stories, they would think, very likely: "Well now, that fable is about me!" and since no one forced them to this thought, they didn't see the lesson underneath and so were not made angry or suspicious. I'll give you an example.

There were two high mountains, and on top of each was a castle. Down in the valley a dog ran sniffing along the ground as if he were looking for something—a mouse or partridge even—to satisfy his hunger. Suddenly, from one of the castles, a trumpet sounded—a sign that dinner was ready. At once the dog began to run up the mountain, hoping to get some scraps; but when he was halfway up the dinner call stopped, and a trumpeting rang out from the other castle. The dog thought: "The first lot will have finished by the time I reach there, but they are only just starting to eat in the other."

So he ran down again and started up the second mountain. But now the first trumpet sounded again and the other one stopped. The dog once more ran down one mountain and up the other, and continued to do this until at last both calls were silent and both meals were over. Poor dog! He was left hungry.

Now you decide what the wise men wished to say in this fable, and whether it is really a dog who runs forth and back, forth and back, changing his mind at every moment and finally getting nowhere?

The Steadfast Tin Soldier

———— Illustrated by ————
Tony Ross

There were once twenty-five tin soldiers, all of them
brothers, for they had been made from the same tin
kitchen spoon. They shouldered arms and looked
straight before them, very smart in their red and blue
uniforms. "Tin soldiers!" That was the very first thing that
they heard in this world, when the lid of their box was taken
off. A little boy had shouted this and clapped his hands; he
had been given them as a birthday present, and now he set
them out on the table. Each soldier was exactly like the
next—except for one, which had only a single leg; he was the
last to be molded, and there was not quite enough tin left.

Yet he stood just as well on his one leg as the others did on their two, and he is this story's hero.

On the table where they were placed there were many other toys, but the one which everyone noticed first was a paper castle. Through its little windows you could see right into the rooms. In front of it, tiny trees were arranged around a piece of mirror, which was meant to look like a lake. Swans made of wax seemed to float on its surface, and gaze at their white reflections. The whole scene was enchanting—and the prettiest thing of all was a girl who stood in the open doorway; she too was cut out of paper, but her gauzy skirt was of finest muslin; a narrow blue ribbon crossed her shoulder like a scarf, and was held by a shining sequin almost the size of her face. This charming little creature held both of her arms stretched out, for she was a dancer; indeed, one of her legs was raised so high in the air that the tin soldier could not see it at all; he thought that she had only one leg like himself.

"Now she would be just the right wife for me," he thought. "But she is so grand. She lives in a castle, and I have only a box—and there are twenty-five of us in that! There certainly isn't room for her. Still, I can try to make her acquaintance." So he lay down full length behind a snuffbox which was on the table; from there he could easily watch the little paper dancer, who continued to stand on one leg without losing her balance.

When evening came, all the other tin soldiers were put in their box, and the children went to bed. Now the toys began to have games of their own; they played at visiting, and schools, and battles, and going to parties. The tin soldiers rattled in their box, for they wanted to join in, but they couldn't get the lid off. The nutcrackers turned somersaults, and the slate pencil squeaked on the slate; there was such a din that the canary woke up and took part in the talk—what's more, he did it in verse. The only two who didn't move were the tin soldier and the little dancer; she continued to stand on the point of her toe, with her arms held out; he stood just as steadily on his single leg—and never once did he take his eyes from her.

Now the clock struck twelve. Crack!—the snuffbox lid flew open and up hopped a little black goblin. There was no snuff in the box—it was a kind of trick, a jack-in-the-box.

"Tin soldier!" screeched the goblin. "Keep your eyes to yourself!"

But the tin soldier pretended not to hear.

"All right, just you wait till tomorrow!" said the goblin.

When morning came and the children were up again, the tin soldier was placed on the window ledge. The goblin may have been responsible, or perhaps a draft blowing through—anyhow, the window suddenly swung open, and out fell the tin soldier, all the three stories to the ground. It was a frightful fall! His leg pointed upwards, his head was down, and he came to a halt with his bayonet stuck between the paving stones.

The servant girl and the little boy went to search in the street, but although they were almost treading on the soldier they somehow failed to see him. If he had called out, "Here I am!" they would have found him easily, but he didn't think it proper behavior to cry out when he was in uniform.

Now it began to rain; the drops fell fast—it was a drenching shower. When it was over, a pair of urchins passed. "Look!" said one of them. "There's a tin soldier. Let's put him out to sea."

So they made a boat out of newspaper and put the tin soldier in the middle, and set it in the fast-flowing gutter at the edge of the street. Away he sped, and the two boys ran beside him clapping their hands. Goodness, what waves there were in that gutter-stream, what rolling tides! It had been a

real downpour. The paper boat tossed up and down, sometimes whirling around and around, until the soldier felt quite giddy. But he remained as steadfast as ever, not moving a muscle, still looking straight in front of him, still shouldering arms.

All at once the boat entered a tunnel under the pavement. Oh, it was dark, quite as dark as it was in the box at home. "Wherever am I going now?" the tin soldier wondered. "Yes, it must be the goblin's doing. Ah! If only that young lady were here with me in the boat, I wouldn't care if it were twice as dark."

Suddenly, from its home in the tunnel, out rushed a large water rat. "Have you a passport?" it demanded. "No entry without a passport!"

But the tin soldier never said a word; he only gripped his musket more tightly than ever. The boat rushed onwards, and behind it rushed the rat in fast pursuit. Ugh! How it ground its teeth, and yelled to the sticks and straws, "Stop him! Stop him! He hasn't paid his toll! He hasn't shown his passport!"

There was no stopping the boat, though, for the stream ran stronger and stronger. The tin soldier could just see a bright glimpse of daylight far ahead where the end of the tunnel must be, but at the same time he heard a roaring noise which well might have frightened a bolder man. Just imagine! At the end of the tunnel the stream thundered down into a great canal. It was as dreadful for him as a plunge down a giant waterfall would be for us.

But how could he stop? Already he was close to the terrible edge. The boat raced on, and the poor tin soldier held himself as stiffly as he could—no one could say of him that he even blinked an eye.

Suddenly the little vessel whirled around three or four times, and filled with water right to the brim; what could it do but sink! The tin soldier stood in water up to his neck; deeper and deeper sank the boat, softer and softer grew the paper, until at last the water closed over the soldier's head. He thought of the lovely little dancer whom he would never see again, and in his ears rang the words of a song:

> *Onward, onward, warrior brave!*
> *Fear not danger, nor the grave.*

Then the paper boat collapsed entirely. Out fell the tin soldier—and he was promptly swallowed up by a fish.

Oh, how dark it was in the fish's stomach! It was even worse than the tunnel, and very much more cramped. But the tin soldier's courage remained unchanged; there he lay, as steadfast as ever, his musket still at his shoulder. The fish swam wildly about, twisted and turned, and then became quite still. Something flashed through like a streak of lightning—then all around was cheerful daylight, and a voice cried out, "The tin soldier!"

The fish had been caught, taken to market, sold and carried into the kitchen, where the cook had cut it open with a large knife. Now she picked up the soldier, holding him around his waist between her finger and thumb, and took him into the living room, so that all the family could see the remarkable character who had traveled about inside a fish. But the tin soldier was not at all proud. They stood him up on the table, and there—well the world is full of wonders!—he saw that he was in the very same room where his adventures had started; there were the very same children; there were the very same toys; there was the fine paper castle with the graceful little dancer at the door. She was still poised on one leg, with the other raised high in the air. Ah, she was steadfast too. The tin soldier was deeply moved; he would have liked to weep tin tears, only that would not have been soldierly behavior. He looked at her, and she looked at him, but not a word passed between them.

And then a strange thing happened. One of the small boys

picked up the tin soldier and threw him into the stove. He had no reason for doing this; it must have been the snuffbox goblin's fault.

The tin soldier stood framed in a blaze of light. The heat was intense, but whether this came from the fire or his burning love, he could not tell. His bright colors were now gone—but whether they had been washed away by his journey, or through his grief, no one could say. He looked at the pretty little dancer, and she looked at him; he felt that he was melting away, but he still stood steadfast, shouldering arms. Suddenly the door flew open; a gust of air caught the little paper girl, and she flew like a sylph right into the stove, straight to the waiting tin soldier; there she flashed into flame and vanished.

The soldier presently melted down to a lump of tin, and the next day, when the maid raked out the ashes, she found him—in the shape of a little tin heart. And the dancer? All they found was her sequin, and that was as black as soot.

From the Ramparts of the Citadel

—————— Illustrated by ——————

Philippe Dupasquier

It is autumn. We are standing on the ramparts of the
citadel, looking out over the sea at the many ships in the
Sound, and at the high Swedish coast beyond, so clear
and sharp in the light of the evening sun. Behind us the
ramparts fall in a steep slope; tall trees rise up from far below;
their yellowing leaves are dropping from the boughs. These
trees overshadow a group of gloomy buildings fenced in by
high wooden walls. Within the fence, where a sentry is pacing
up and down, it is bleak and cheerless enough, but behind
the iron-barred holes in the walls there are cells which are
even more dark and grim. Here the worst criminals are
imprisoned.

Into one of these bare cells comes a ray from the setting
sun. The sun shines on the evil as well as the good! The

51

prisoner looks with hate at the thin cold beam, too weak to bring him warmth or joy. A little bird flutters down and alights on the iron bars. Yes, the bird sings both for the wicked and the good! It trills out only a few notes—tirria! tirria!—but it does not fly away. It preens itself, plucks a feather, ruffles its wings—and the tormented man in chains watches it. A dreaming look crosses the rough, scarcely human face; a feeling passes through him, one that he neither knows nor understands. Yet it is linked with the sunbeam, with the bird, with the smell of violets, growing richly in the dank earth outside.

Now a hunting horn sounds from the wood, so thrilling and strong. The bird flies away from the prison bars; the sun's ray disappears. All is dark again in the cell, and in the heart of the evil man. Yet the sun has shone into that darkness, if only for a moment, and the voice of the bird has touched it too.

Sound on, you haunting music from the horn in the woods! As we gaze from the ramparts the evening is so mild; the sea is smooth as a mirror, and as calm.

The Swineherd

——————— Illustrated by ———————

Jutta Ash

There once was a poor Prince. He had a kingdom which was really quite small; but whatever its size, it was big enough to marry on, and that's what he meant to do. Now some might think it was bold of him to say to the Emperor's daughter, "Will you have me?" But bold he was, and dare he did. After all, he had a very good reputation himself as a prince, and there were hundreds of princesses who would have said, "Yes please!" But did this one? She did not. Now listen, and you'll know what really happened.

On the grave of the Prince's father a rose tree grew. What a beautiful tree it was! It flowered only once every five years, and even then it had only one flower. But that was a rose so sweet and fragrant that if you were lucky enough to catch a whiff of its scent, all your griefs and troubles would disappear. He also owned a nightingale which could sing as if

54

all the loveliest melodies in the world lived in its voice. The Prince decided to send the rose and the nightingale to the Emperor's daughter. They were placed in fine silver caskets and carried to the palace.

The Emperor ordered the gifts to be brought before him into the hall where the princess was playing "Let's go visiting" with her maids-of-honor. That was all they ever did! But when she saw the pretty silver containers with presents for her inside she clapped her hands for joy.

"Oh, I do hope it's a little pussycat!" she cried as the first was opened. But it was the Prince's rose.

"It's very nicely made," said one of the ladies-in-waiting.

"It's more than nice," said the Emperor. "I would call it a handsome item, quite remarkable."

But when the Princess touched it, she wanted to cry.

"Oh, Papa," she said. "It's not made at all, it's only real!"

"What a shame!" said all the maids-of-honor. "It's only real!"

"Now, now, let's see what's in the other box before we start complaining," said the Emperor. Then out came the nightingale. She sang so sweetly that for a few moments no one could think of anything bad to say.

"*Superbe! Charmant!*" exclaimed the maids-of-honor, for they all spoke French, each one worse than the next.

"How this bird reminds me of the late Empress's musical box," said an old courtier. "Why, yes, it's the same tone exactly, the same expression!"

"Yes, you are right," said the Emperor, and he cried like a child.

"Are you sure that's a real bird?" asked the Princess.

"Oh, yes, that's a real bird all right," said one of the men who had brought it.

"Then it can fly off for all I care," said the Princess. And she refused to let the Prince into the palace.

But he was not to be put off so easily. He smeared his face brown and black, pulled a cap down over his eyes and knocked at the front door.

"Good morning, Emperor," he said. "Do you happen to have a job for me in your palace?"

"Well, we get so many requests," said the Emperor. "But wait—I could do with someone to look after the pigs. We've got so many of them."

And so the Prince was taken on as Imperial Swineherd. He was given a dirty little hut next to the pigsty, and there he was expected to live. But he worked away all day long, and by evening he had made a charming little cooking pot. All around it were tiny bells, and as soon as the pot began to boil they would tinkle away so prettily, playing the old tune:

> *Ah, my dearest Augustin,*
> *All's gone, gone, gone.*

But the strangest thing about it was that if you held your finger in the steam you could straightway smell what was being cooked for dinner on every stove in town. Well, that was quite a different thing from the rose.

Now the Princess was taking a stroll with her young ladies, but when she heard the tinkling tune she stopped. She looked pleased. "Ah, my dearest Augustin"—she could play that tune. In fact, it was the only tune that she *could* play, and she did it with one finger.

"I know that tune!" she said. "It's my tune! I can play it! He must be a very well-educated swineherd. Go and ask him the price of his instrument."

And so one of the girls had to run up and ask. But she put on her clogs first, to keep her feet from the mud.

"How much do you want for that pot?" asked the girl.

"I want ten kisses from the Princess," said the Swineherd.

"Goodness gracious!" said the maid-of-honor.

"Ten and no less, that's my price," said the Swineherd.

"Quick—what did he say?" asked the Princess.

"I really can't tell you," said the maid-of-honor. "It's too shocking."

"Then whisper it to me," said the Princess. So the girl whispered it.

"What a rude fellow!" said the Princess. And she briskly walked away.

But she had gone only a few steps when the bells rang out again, tinkling their sweet tune:

Ah, my dearest Augustin,
All's gone, gone, gone.

"Listen," said the Princess. "Ask him if he will take ten kisses from my ladies-in-waiting."

"Thank you, no," said the Swineherd. "Ten kisses from the Princess, or I keep my musical pot."

"How tiresome he is," said the Princess. "But if I do, you girls must stand around me, so that no one sees."

Thereupon the ladies-in-waiting gathered around, and spread out their skirts. Then the Swineherd got his kisses and the Princess got the pot.

And now the fun began. All that evening and the whole of the next day the pot was kept on the boil; there wasn't a single oven in town that could keep to itself what was being cooked inside, whether it was the Lord High Chamberlain's or the shoemaker's. The young ladies-in-waiting danced about for joy and clapped their hands.

"We know who's going to have soup and pancakes! We know who's going to have roast meat and rice pudding!" they cried. "It's so interesting!"

"Indeed, most interesting," murmured the palace housekeeper.

"Be careful though," said the Princess. "Don't breathe a word to anyone. Remember—I'm the Emperor's daughter."

"We wouldn't dream of telling," they all said.

The Swineherd (that is to say, the Prince, but they had no idea that he wasn't a real Swineherd) never let a day pass without inventing something. Now he made a rattle; when it was swung around it played all the waltzes, jigs and polkas ever known.

"But that is *superbe*," cried the Princess as she passed. "I've never heard such fascinating music. I say, do go in, one of you, and ask him how much he wants for the rattle. But mind, no kissing."

"He wants a hundred kisses from the Princess," the maid-of-honor reported when she returned.

"He must be mad," said the Princess, and walked on. But when she had gone only a little way, she stopped. "We must do all we can to encourage the arts!" she said. "After all, I am the Emperor's daughter. Tell him that he may have ten kisses, the same as yesterday. The rest will come from my ladies-in-waiting."

"Oh, we wouldn't like that," said the girls.

"Stuff and nonsense!" said the Princess. "If I can kiss him, so can you. Besides—why do you think I pay your board and wages?"

And so the maid-of-honor had to go back with the message.

"A hundred kisses from the Princess," said the Swineherd. "Or we each keep what's our own."

"Oh well," said the Princess. "But stand around closely."

So the girls stood closely around her and the kissing began.

"Whatever is going on by the pigsty?" said the Emperor, who had just stepped on to the balcony. He rubbed his eyes and put on his spectacles. "Those maids-of-honor are up to some mischief, I'll be bound; I'd better go down and see."

And he pulled his slippers up at the back. They were old ones, you understand, and were trodden down at the heel. Goodness, how he hurried! But once he was in the courtyard, he crept along, step by step, so as not to make a sound. The maids-of-honor were so busy counting the kisses, to see that all was fair, that none of them noticed the Emperor. He stood on tiptoe, to see over their heads.

"What's going on?" he demanded. But when he saw his daughter busily kissing his Swineherd, he swiped them over the head with his slipper, just as the young man was having his eighty-sixth kiss.

"Get out, both of you!" roared the Emperor. Oh, he was furious! And so the Princess and the Swineherd were banished from the kingdom.

There she stood crying, while the Swineherd scolded her, and the rain poured down.

"Oh, how unhappy I am," said the Princess. "If only I had accepted the handsome Prince! I'm so miserable!"

Then the Swineherd went behind a tree, cleaned the black and brown from his face, threw off his rough clothes and stepped forward dressed as a prince. He looked so handsome and splendid that the Princess actually curtsied.

"I've learned what you are worth, my dear," he said. "You turned down an honest prince. You despised a living rose, and a living nightingale. But a swineherd could win your kisses for a toy, a musical box. Now you must do what you can."

Then he stepped into his kingdom, and shut and bolted the door.

Left standing there outside, what could she do but sing the one song she knew:

Ah, my dearest Augustin,
All's gone, gone, gone.

The Little Match Girl

———— Illustrated by ————

Ralph Steadman

It was dreadfully cold. Snow was falling; soon it would be quite dark. It was also the very last evening of the year— New Year's Eve. In this cold and darkness, a poor little girl was wandering along, with bare head and bare feet. It's true that she had slippers on when she left home—but what good was that? They were great big things, those slippers; they had belonged to her mother, so it is not surprising that they had fallen off when she scurried across the road just missing two carts that were thundering past. One slipper was nowhere to be found, and a boy ran off with the other. It would do for a cradle when he had children of his own, he called out teasingly.

So there was the little girl treading along on naked feet that were quite blue with cold. In an old apron she carried a pile of matches, and she held one bunch of them in her hand. She had sold nothing the whole of the day; no one had given her a single penny. Hungry and frozen she trudged along looking so miserable. Poor little thing! The snowflakes fell on her long fair hair that curled so prettily at her neck. But she certainly wasn't thinking about her looks. Lights were shining in every window and wonderful smells of roasting goose drifted down the street. For it was New Year's Eve, remember, and that's what she was thinking about.

In a sheltered corner between two houses, one jutting out a little further than the other, she crouched down and huddled herself together, tucking up her legs—but this didn't help; she grew colder and colder. She didn't dare to go home, for she had sold no matches. She hadn't a single copper coin to bring back and so her father would beat her. Besides, her home was freezing too. It was an attic under the roof, and the wind whistled through that, though the worst cracks had been stuffed with straw and rags.

Her hands were quite numb with cold. A match flame would be such a comfort. Oh, if only she dared to strike one match, just one. She took one and struck it against the wall—crrritch! How it crackled and blazed! What a lovely warm clear flame, just like a little candle! She held her hand around it. Really, it was a wonderful light. The little girl seemed to be sitting in front of a big iron stove with shining brass knobs and fittings; inside was such a warm friendly fire. Oh, what had happened? She had just put out her toes to warm them too when—the flame went out. The stove had gone! She was sitting in the cold with the stump of a burnt-out matchstick in her hand.

She struck another match. It flared up brightly; where it shone, the wall became transparent as gauze. She could see right into the room where the table was laid with a shining starched white cloth; on it were dishes of finest porcelain. A delicious hot fragrance rose from a roast goose stuffed with prunes and apples. The goose seemed nearer and nearer—she could almost touch it. Then the match went out. All she could see and feel was the cold unfriendly wall.

She struck another. Now she was sitting under the loveliest of Christmas trees, even bigger and more beautifully decorated than the great tree she had seen at Christmas through the glass door of the rich merchant's shop. Thousands of candles were alight on its branches, and brightly colored Christmas pictures, just like the ones in all the shop windows, were looking down at her kindly. The little girl reached out her hands—then the match burned out. But the flames from the candles seemed to rise higher and higher, and she saw that they were the stars in the heavens, high above. One of them rushed across, leaving a fiery streak in the dark night sky.

"Someone is dying!" said the little girl. Her grandmother, now dead, the only person who had ever been kind to her, had told her once that whenever a star falls, it is a sign that a soul is going to God.

She struck another match on the wall. As it lit up the blackness all around, she saw in its bright glow her dear grandmother. How sweet she looked, so loving and so kind.

"Oh Granny, take me with you," she cried. "I know you'll disappear when the match goes out, just like the warm stove and the roast goose and the wonderful Christmas tree!" And without stopping she struck all the rest of the matches in the bundle. Her grandmother must not go!

The flames shone out so brilliantly that all around was even brighter than daylight. Never before had her grandmother looked so tall and beautiful. She took the little girl in her arms and flew with her in joy and splendor up and up to where there is no cold, no fear, no hunger—up to heaven.

In the cold early morning, huddled in a corner, there sat the little girl, with red cheeks and smiling lips—frozen to death on the last night of the old year. The New Year dawned on the little dead body with its lapful of matches; one bundle was burnt out. "She was trying to warm herself," people said. No one knew what lovely things she had seen, and how gloriously she had flown with her grandmother into her own New Year.

The Top and the Ball

———— Illustrated by ————

Fulvio Testa

The Top and the Ball lay in the same drawer with a number of other toys. One day the Top said to the Ball, "Why shouldn't we be sweethearts? After all, we are neighbors; we live in the same drawer." But the Ball was made of morocco leather and fancied herself as a very superior young lady, and she couldn't be bothered to answer a question like that.

Next day in came the little boy who owned the toys. He painted the Top red and gold and hammered a bright brass nail down the middle. The Top looked quite magnificent, especially when spinning around. "Just see me now!" he said to the Ball. "Well, what about it? Shouldn't we be sweethearts? We make a proper pair! You can jump and I can dance. We'd be the happiest couple in the world!"

"That's what you think," said the Ball. "Clearly you don't know that my mother and father were real morocco leather slippers. What's more, I have a cork inside me!"

"Yes, but I am made of the best mahogany," said the Top. "And that's not all—the Mayor himself made me on his lathe;

he had one in his home. He was very pleased with me, I tell you that."

"Do you expect me to believe your story?" said the Ball.

"May I never be spun again if I'm telling a lie!" said the Top.

"You speak up well for yourself, I must say that," said the Ball. "But I can't accept your offer—I'm as good as engaged to a Swallow. Every time I leap into the air he puts his head out of the nest and says, 'Will you? Will you?' I haven't exactly said yes, but I've thought it in my mind, and that makes us quite halfway to being engaged. But I promise I shall never forget you."

"Much use that will be!" said the Top. And there the conversation ended.

Next day the Ball was taken outside. The Top watched her flying into the air like a bird, higher and higher each time until she was quite out of sight. Whenever she came down and hit the ground she bounced up again, high, high, high; that was because she wished to advance in the world, or maybe because she had a cork inside. The ninth time she went up she never came back. The boy searched and searched, but she had gone.

"I could tell them where she is," sighed the Top. "She is in the Swallow's nest. She's marrying the Swallow."

The more the Top thought about the Ball the more he missed her, the more he longed for her. And just because he could not have her, he loved her all the more. It was so strange, so puzzling that she had chosen someone else. The Top whirled around and around, around and around, and all the time his thoughts were on the Ball. In his mind she grew more and more beautiful. Years went by, and then at last his passion became just a memory, a long-ago love affair.

By now the Top wasn't young either. But one day he was painted gold all over. Never had he looked so handsome! He

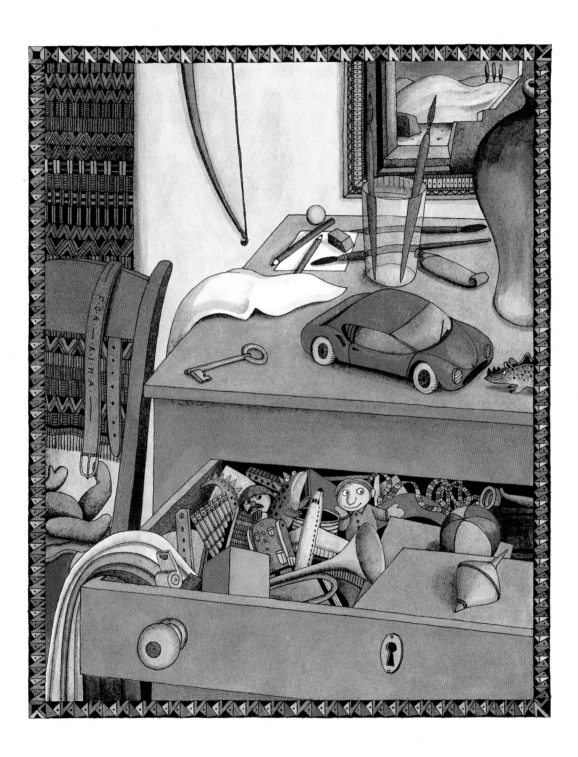

had become a golden Top, and he whirled and danced until the air hummed about him. Then suddenly he skipped too high, and was gone.

Everyone looked everywhere, even in the cellar, but he was nowhere to be found. Where could he be?

He had jumped into the rubbish bin, a very low place where all kinds of things were lying—cabbage stalks, sweepings, dirt and dead leaves from the gutter under the roof.

Well, this is a fine place to be in! My gold coat won't last long. And the company here, such riff raff! He looked out of the corner of his eye at a very bare cabbage stalk, and at an odd round thing which might have been a rotten apple. Only, it wasn't an apple; it was an old ball which had lain for years in the wet and dirty gutter.

"Thank goodness, here's someone of my own class to talk to," said the Ball as she saw the golden Top. "I must tell you that I am made of morocco leather, stitched by a young lady's hand. I have a cork inside me too, though you might not think it to look at me. I was just going to marry a swallow when I fell into the gutter and there I lay in the sopping wet for five years. That's a long time for a young lady, I can tell you!"

But the Top said nothing. He was thinking of his lost sweetheart, and the more she prattled on the more certain he became that this was she.

Soon the maid came along to empty the dustbin. "Oh, hurray!" she cried. "Here's the golden Top!"

The Top went back to its honored place in the house. But no one remembered the Ball and nothing more was ever heard of her. The Top never mentioned his former love again. It's hard to feel the same when your sweetheart has spent five years in a sopping wet gutter. In fact, you don't recognize her if you meet in a rubbish bin.

The Princess and the Pea

Illustrated by

Inga Moore

There was once a prince who wished to marry a princess—but a real princess she had to be. So he traveled all the world over to find one; yet in every case something was wrong. Princesses were there in plenty, yet he could never be sure that they were the genuine article; there was always something, this or that, that just didn't seem as it should be. At last he came back home, quite downhearted, for he did so want to have a real princess.

One evening there was a fearful storm; thunder raged, lightning flashed, rain poured down in torrents—it was horrifying. In the midst of it all, someone knocked at the palace door, and the old King went to open it.

Standing there was a princess. But, goodness! What a state she was in! The water ran down her hair and her clothes, through the tips of her shoes and out at the heels. Still, she *said* she was a real princess.

"Well, we'll find out soon enough," the old Queen thought. She didn't say a word, though, but went into the spare bedroom, took off all the bedclothes, and laid a little pea on the mattress. Then she piled up twenty more mattresses on top of it, and twenty quilts over that. There the Princess was to sleep that night.

When morning came, they asked her how she had slept.

"Oh, shockingly! Not a wink of sleep the whole night long! Heaven knows what was in the bed, but I lay on something hard that has made me black and blue all over. It was unspeakable."

Now they were sure that here was a real princess, since she had felt the pea through twenty quilts and twenty mattresses. Only a real princess could be so sensitive.

So the Prince married her; no need to search any further. The pea was put in the museum; you can go and see it for yourself if no one has taken it.

There's a fine story for you!

The Flying Trunk

———— Illustrated by ————
Satoshi Kitamura

T here was once a merchant who was so rich that he could have paved the whole street with silver, and still have had nearly enough over for a little alley way as well. But that isn't what he did with his money—Oh no, he had more sense. Whenever he laid out a penny it brought him ten: that's the kind of merchant he was. And then he died.

All his money now came to his son—and he lost no time in spending it. Every night he went out dancing; he made paper kites from bank notes; he played ducks and drakes on the lake—not with flat stones, but with gold coins. That's the way to run through money, and very soon he had nothing left but four copper coins and the clothes he had on, which were an old dressing gown and a pair of slippers. Needless to say, his friends all drifted off: who would wish to be seen with such a ragamuffin? But one of them, more good-natured than the rest, gave him an old trunk, saying,

"You'll be moving off, I fancy. That's for your luggage." All very well, but he had no luggage. So he put himself in the trunk.

It was no ordinary trunk. As soon as you pressed the lock, it rose from the ground and flew. The young man pressed the lock and—swoosh!—the trunk was taking him up through the chimney, over the clouds, higher and higher, further and further away. The bottom creaked and groaned—what if it fell out? No acrobatics could help him then. But the trunk held together, and landed at last in the country of the Turks. He hid it under some leaves in a wood, and walked towards the town.

Nobody took any notice of him because all the Turks go about in dressing gowns and slippers. He met a nursemaid with a young child. "I say, nanny," he called out, "what's the great palace just outside the city, with the windows so high in the walls?"

"Oh, that's where the king's daughter lives," she answered. "A fortune teller has prophesied that she's going to have an unhappy love affair. So no one is allowed to visit her unless the king and queen are there as well."

"Thank you," said the merchant's son. He hurried back to the wood, stepped into his trunk and flew up, on to the palace roof. Then he climbed through the window of the princess's room. It was quite easy!

She was fast asleep on a sofa, and looked so beautiful that the merchant's son couldn't help giving her a kiss. This woke her up. Oh, she was frightened to see a strange young man bending over her. But he explained that he was a Turkish god, and had come flying down from the sky to call on her. She liked that story.

Then they sat side by side, and he told her tales about her eyes; they were deep and lovely lakes, he said, and her thoughts swam through them like mermaids. He told her about her forehead; it was a snowy mountain, but inside were wonderful rooms and galleries, with the loveliest pictures on the walls. And he told her about the stork, which flies in with charming little babies—tales of that kind. And then he asked her to marry him, and she said yes.

"But you must come here on Saturday," she said. "That's when my parents, the king and queen, will be having tea with me. They *will* be proud that I am going to marry a Turkish god. But do be sure to tell them some good stories; they'll enjoy that so much. Only, my mother likes tales with a moral, very proper, you know, while Father prefers something lively, to make him laugh."

"Very well," said the merchant's son. "A story shall be my wedding present."

So they parted, but the princess gave him a sword which was decorated with gold coins. He had plenty of use for those.

Off he flew, and bought himself a new dressing gown. Then he sat down in the wood to think about his story. It had to be ready by Saturday, and that isn't so easy. But at last it was finished, and Saturday had arrived.

The king and queen and all the court were at the tea party, waiting for him to come. They gave him a charming welcome.

"Now, do tell us a story," said the queen. "But mind, it must have a serious moral."

"Yes, yes, but you must make us laugh as well," said the king.

"I'll do my best," said the young man, and he began his story. "Now, listen carefully."

"Once upon a time there was a bundle of matches. They were extremely proud and haughty because they came of such high beginnings. Their family tree—the one they had all been part of—was once a tall and ancient pine tree in the forest. Now the matches lay on a kitchen shelf between a tinderbox and an old iron pot, and they told these neighbors all about the time when they were young.

"'Ah yes,' they said, 'we were on the top of the world when we were on that tree. Every morning and evening we had diamond tea—they call it dew—and all day we had sunshine (when there *was* any sunshine) and all the little birds had to tell us stories. We could easily see that we were grander than the rest; we could afford green clothes all the year round, while the poor oaks and beeches wore leaves only in summer time . . . .

"'But then the woodcutter came—we call it the Great Revolution—and the family was split up. Our mighty trunk found a place as the mainmast of a great ship which could sail around the world if she'd a mind to. Jobs of various kinds were found for the branches, and we were appointed to bring light to the lower orders. You must be wondering how such highborn persons as ourselves came to be in this kitchen. Now you know.'

"'I have a different history,' said the iron pot. 'Ever since I first came into the world I have been scrubbed and boiled, boiled and scrubbed—I can't count the number of times. I do the solid work here, the only kind that matters. Strictly speaking, I'm the Number One person in this house. What do I most enjoy? I'll tell you. It's to settle down on this shelf, clean and tidy, when all the business of dinner is over, and have a sensible chat with friends. Except for the water bucket, which goes into the yard now and then, we all prefer to stay at home. None of that foreign travel for us. The only one who brings in news is the shopping basket. But it's wild, disagreeable stuff, always about the government and the people. Why! Only the other day an elderly jug in this kitchen was so shaken by what the basket said that he fell down and broke into pieces. Yes, he was absolutely shattered. Yes, she's a real troublemaker, that basket; I wouldn't trust her politics at all.'

"'You do ramble on,' growled the tinderbox, and it

clashed its flint and steel to give out sparks. 'I was hoping for a livelier evening.'

"'Yes,' said the matches, 'we do need brightening up. What about discussing which of us comes from the best family? That would be interesting.'

"'No, I don't like talking about myself,' said an earthenware pot. 'Let's do something more entertaining. For a start I'll tell you a story, the kind we can all enter into. Right? On the Baltic shores, where the Danish beech trees wave their boughs—'

"'What a fine beginning!' said the plates. 'We like that story already.'

"'Well,' continued the earthenware pot, 'it was there that I spent my youth, in a very respectable household. The furniture was polished every week, the floors washed every day, and clean curtains were put up every two weeks.'

"'You make it all sound so interesting,' said the broom. 'Anyone can tell you're a lady. Your story is so clean and refined.'

"'Yes, I thought that too,' said the water bucket, and it gave a hop and skip of pleasure, plink! plop!—on the kitchen floor. The pot went on with her story, and the end was just as good as the beginning. The plates all clattered together—that was their way of showing applause—while the broom took some parsley from the dustbin and put it around the pot like a crown; he knew that this would annoy the others. 'If I crown her today,' he thought, 'she'll crown me tomorrow.'

"'Now I'm going to dance,' said the tongs, and dance she did. My, my, how high she could kick her legs! The old chintz chair cover split right down the middle trying to get a good view. 'Where's my crown?' the tongs demanded when the dance was done. So she was crowned as well.

"'A common, vulgar lot,' thought the matches, but they kept the thought to themselves.

"The big tea urn was asked to sing, but she had a cold, she said; unless she was on the boil she wasn't in good voice. The truth was that she was too conceited and proud to sing in the kitchen. She would only perform in the dining room when the master and mistress were present.

"Over on the window ledge was an old quill pen that the maid servant used. There was nothing special about her except the fact that she had been dipped too deep in the ink-well. This seemed to the pen a mark of distinction, and she was quite vain about it. 'If the tea urn doesn't wish to sing,' said the pen, 'why should we try to make her? There's a nightingale outside; she can manage a few notes. It's true that she has never had lessons—the bird is quite uneducated—but let's not be fussy tonight.'

" 'I don't approve at all,' said the kettle. She was the kitchen's chief vocalist; she was also half sister to the tea urn. 'Why should we listen to a foreign bird? Is it patriotic? I put it to the shopping basket—don't you think I am right?'

" 'I'm really disappointed,' said the basket. 'Is this the proper way to spend an evening, squabbling and squabbling? Wouldn't it be better to set our house in order? Let us start by putting everyone in his or her proper place. That, of course, will set me at the top; I'll be in charge. You'll see a few changes!'

" 'Yes, why not?' said the dishes. 'We could do with a little stirring up.'

"But at that moment the door opened. It was the maid. Not one of them moved; not one of them made a sound. Yet every single pot in the place was silently telling itself how gifted it really was, how much above the rest in style and quality. 'Given the chance,' each thought, 'I could have made a real success of the evening.'

"The maid picked up the matches and struck them. How they spluttered and blazed! 'Now,' they thought, 'everyone can see that we are the top people here. No one can shine like us—what brilliance! What a light we throw on dark places!'

"And then they were all burnt out."

"That was a lovely tale!" said the queen. "I feel as if I had been in the kitchen all the time, especially with those matches. You shall certainly marry our daughter."

"Yes, yes, of course," said the king. "We'll have the wedding on Monday." And he dropped his royal manner when he spoke, since the young man was now one of the family.

Everything was arranged, and on the eve of the wedding the whole city was lit up. Cakes and buns were thrown to be scrambled for; the street urchins hopped about on tiptoe, cheering and whistling through their fingers. It was a glorious occasion. Just to be there was enough to make anyone happy.

"I suppose I ought to be doing something too," thought the merchant's son. So he bought rockets and whizzbangs, every kind of firework you could think of. Then he put them into his trunk and flew up into the air. Swoosh! Bang! How those fireworks blazed and thundered! All the Turks were leaping into the air with the wonder of it; their slippers were flying about their ears. Never in their lives had they seen such a fantastic show. Now they were certain that the princess was marrying a real Turkish god.

As soon as the merchant's son reached the wood he thought he would go back to the town to hear for himself what the people were saying about his fiery flight. You might have done the same yourself—it was perfectly natural. Goodness, how they were talking! Every person had a different version of the happening, but they all thought it magical.

"I saw the Turkish god himself," said one. "He had eyes like glittering stars, and a beard like the rolling waves!"

"He wore a great cloak of fire," said another. "I saw cherubs peeping from the folds—lovely little things they were."

Oh yes, there was plenty of good listening for the young man. And next day was to be his wedding day

At last he went back to the wood to get his trunk—but what had become of it? The trunk was burnt to cinders. A spark from the fireworks had set it alight, and all that remained was ashes. He could not fly; so he could not get back to his bride.

All day she stood waiting on the roof. She is waiting still. As for him, he goes wandering around the world, on foot, telling fairy tales. But somehow none is as lighthearted as the one he told of the matches.